Yellow Moon

Groundwood Books
House of Anansi Press
TORONTO   BERKELEY

Apple Moon

Pamela Porter

Matt James

Yellow Moon, Apple Moon,
Time to sleep. See you soon.

Here's my house, my swing, my tree.

Here's my window, my bed and me.

Here's my pillow, Here's my head.
Here's the book my daddy read.

Here's my kitty, soft and dear.
Here's my arm to hold her near.

Is that Mommy's song I hear?

There's my window,
swing and tree.
My cat waits there
by the door
for me.

There the robins snuggle tight.

Here my mommy sings good night.

At the gate of heaven little shoes they are selli

For the little barefooted angels there dwelling.

Slumber, my baby, slumber, my baby,
Slumber, my baby,
Slumber, my baby, arru, arru.

Yellow Moon, Apple Moon,

Time to sleep. See you soon.

At the Gate of Heaven

At the gate of heaven little shoes they are selling,
For the little barefooted angels there dwelling.
Slumber, my baby, slumber, my baby,
Slumber, my baby, arru, arru.

God will bless children so peacefully sleeping,
God will help the mothers whose love they are keeping.
Slumber, my baby, slumber, my baby,
Slumber, my baby, arru, arru.

A la puerta del cielo

A la puerta del cielo venden zapatos,
Para los angelitos que andan descalzos.
Duérmete, niño(a), duérmete, niño(a),
Duérmete, niño(a), arrú, arrú.

A los niños que duermen Dios los bendice,
A las madres que velan Dios las asiste.
Duérmete, niño(a), duérmete, niño(a),
Duérmete, niño(a), arrú, arrú.

At the Gate of Heaven • *A la puerta del cielo*

1. At the gate of heav'n lit - tle shoes they are sell - ing,
A la puer - ta del cie - lo ven - den za - pa - tos,

For the lit - tle bare - foot - ed an - gels there dwell - ing.
Pa - ra los an - ge - li - tos que an - dan des - cal - zos.

Divisi*

Slum - ber, my ba - by, Slum - ber, my ba - by,
Duér - me - te, ni - ño, Duér - me - te, ni - ño,

Ah_____ , Ah_____ ,

Melody

Slum - ber, my ba - by, a - rru, a - rru.
Duér - me - te, ni - ño, a - rrú, a - rrú.

*Divisi means that the high voices divide to sing two upper parts while the low voices continue their one part.

Groundwood Books / House of Anansi Press
110 Spadina Avenue, Suite 801, Toronto, Ontario M5V 2K4
Distributed in the USA by Publishers Group West
1700 Fourth Street, Berkeley, CA 94710

We acknowledge for their financial support of our publishing
program the Canada Council for the Arts, the Government of
Canada and the Ontario Arts Council.

Canada Council   Conseil des Arts
for the Arts   du Canada

ONTARIO ARTS COUNCIL
CONSEIL DES ARTS DE L'ONTARIO
an Ontario government agency
un organisme du gouvernement de l'Ontario

With the participation of the government of Canada
Avec la participation du gouvernement du Canada | Canadä

Library and Archives Canada Cataloguing in Publication
Porter, Pamela Paige
Yellow moon, apple moon / Pamela Porter ; illustrated by
Matt James.
ISBN 978-0-88899-809-5
I. James, Matt II. Title.
PS8581.O7573Y44 2008   jC813'.6   C2007-903293-1

The illustrations are in acrylic and India ink on panel.
Designed by Michael Solomon
Printed and bound in Malaysia

FSC
www.fsc.org
MIX
Paper from
responsible sources
FSC® C012700